The Nap Master

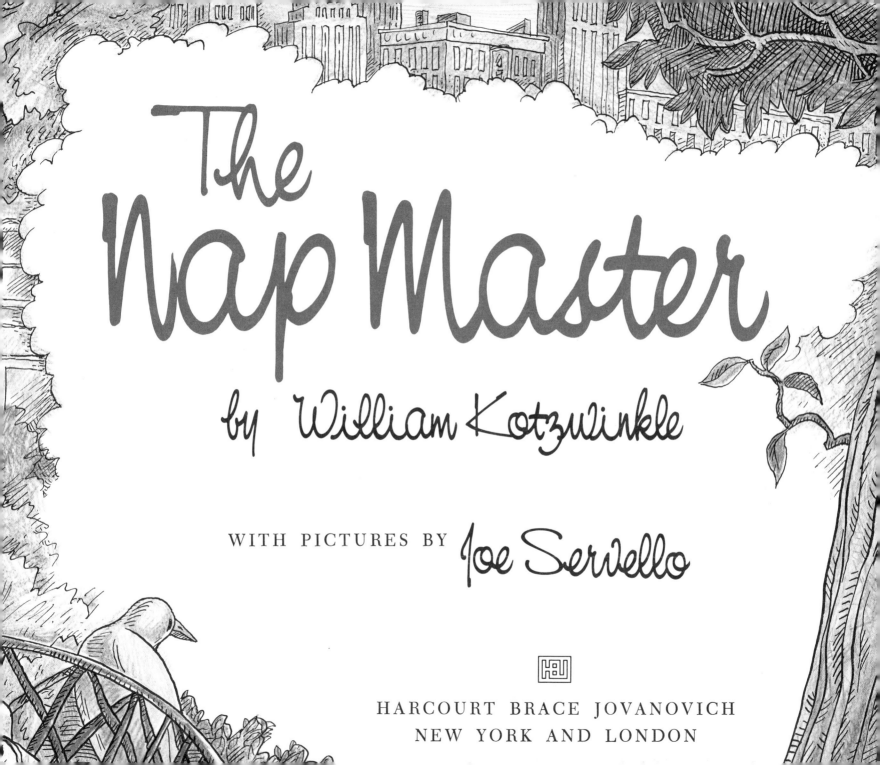

The Nap Master

by William Kotzwinkle

WITH PICTURES BY Joe Servello

HARCOURT BRACE JOVANOVICH
NEW YORK AND LONDON

Library of Congress Cataloging in Publication Data

Kotzwinkle, William.
The nap master

SUMMARY: Herman refuses to take a nap until the Nap
Master takes a hand.
[1. Sleep—Fiction]   I. Servello, Joe.   II. Title.
PZ7.K855   Nap   [E]   78-12178
ISBN 0-15-256704-6
ISBN 0-15-665325-7 pbk.

First edition

B C D E

*Other Children's Books by
William Kotzwinkle and Joe Servello*
The Firemen
The Ship That Came Down the Gutter
The Oldest Man and Other Timeless Stories
The Day the Gang Got Rich
Elephant Boy
The Return of Crazy Horse
The Supreme, Superb, Exalted and Delightful,
One and Only Magic Building
Up the Alley with Jack and Joe
The Leopard's Tooth
The Ants Who Took Away Time

"I am the Nap Master. You put an ad in the newspaper?"
"Please come in. Though I'm afraid it won't do much good.
Nobody can make Herman take his nap."

"I won't take a nap. I don't ever take naps. NAPS ARE FOR SAPS!"
said Herman.

The Nap Master sat down on the floor beside him and stretched himself out. "You don't mind if I catch a few winks, do you?"

"Do what you like," said Herman. "But I have more important things to do. NAPS ARE FOR SAPS!"

The Nap Master began to snore, strange noises coming from his lips.
"Honk. . . . Wheeze. . . . Tiggle. . . . Booof. . . ."

Herman was furious! "NAPS ARE FOR SAPS!" he said, and he ran into
the hall to play with his friend the elevator man.

"Elevator man! I'm pressing all the buttons!"

But the elevator man didn't see. He was taking a nap.

The elevator stopped at every floor. No one got on because everyone else was napping, too.

Herman rode sadly down to the basement.

"Cleaning man, I'm tipping over your bucket."

The cleaning man just snored.

"Maintenance man, I'm sawing the leg off your chair. . . ."

The maintenance man went ZZZZ-ZZZZZZZZ.

"Doorman, doorman," called Herman. "Doorman, look at me!"
Herman raced around in the revolving doors, pushing them as fast as he could.

The doorman didn't see. He was taking a nap.

Herman rode sadly back upstairs.
His mother was napping. The Nap
Master was napping. Even Polly
the parrot was napping.

He sat down in the big stuffed chair in his playroom.

Herman's eyelids started to droop. His toes got limp.
His legs felt like melted butter. His head became very, very heavy.

"Honk. . . . Wheeze. . . . Tiggle. . . . Booof," said Herman.

Herman was asleep.

And there inside his dream was the Nap Master.

"What took you so long?" asked the Nap Master.
"Come with me and I'll show you the sights."
They went walking down a winding road to a stream.

"Now here," said the Nap Master, "is how you run on the water."
They jumped onto the stream and went skating away, making circles
and spin-abouts, and took a great sliding turn into the harbor, where
the Dream Stream met the sea.

They skated in among the ships, spraying water with their sliding feet. Herman skated in back of an evil-looking ship, with cannons peeking from its hull and a skull-and-crossbones flying from its mast.

A pirate reached out and snatched him up!

"Nap Master!" shouted Herman. "Help me!"

But the pirate ship was sailing from the bay into the
Ocean of Dreams.

Herman kicked and squirmed, but the pirate just dumped him on the deck and scowled at him wickedly.

"Doorman!" cried Herman. "What are you doing here?"

"*Ask to polish his buttons, polish his buttons. Squawk, squawk!*"

Herman looked up and saw Polly hanging from the mast.

"Let me polish the buttons on your fine jacket, sir,"
said Herman to the doorman-pirate.

"All right, get busy. But no tricks." The pirate threw
his jacket to Herman, and Herman polished with all his might.
The buttons began to shine so brightly that the pirate's eyes were
blinded by the glow.

Herman raced off across the deck, but he tripped on a pail of water and sent it flying.

"Why, you clumsy little cod!" shouted another pirate, who was cleaning the deck. He swung his mop at Herman's head.

"Cleaning man!" shouted Herman. "It's me, Herman Corderinkle!"

Herman jumped inside a coil of rope, where a tiny sea shell lay glistening. Snoring sounds came from inside it.

"Honk. . . . Wheeze. . . . Tiggle. . . . Booof. . . . Burble. . . ."

"Nap Master!"

"This way," said the Nap Master, pulling Herman by the hand down into the shell.

Through the curving spirals of the shell they raced, around and down, to the very bottom.

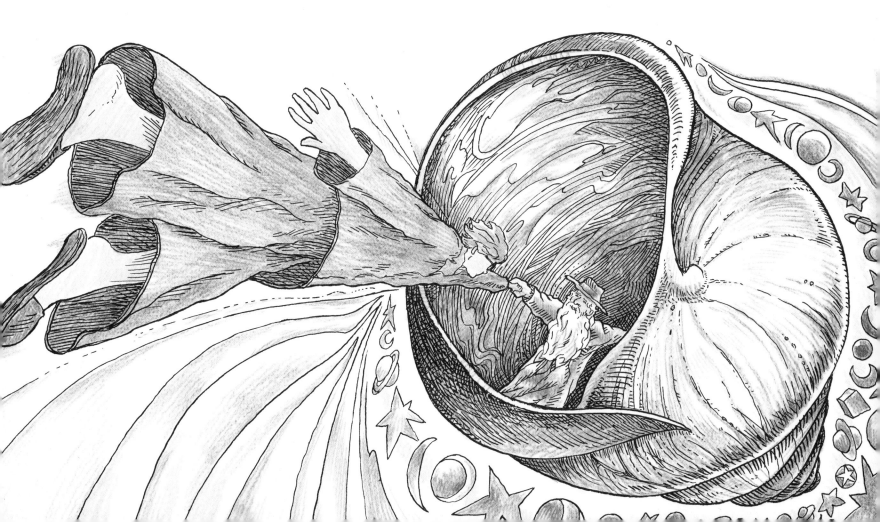

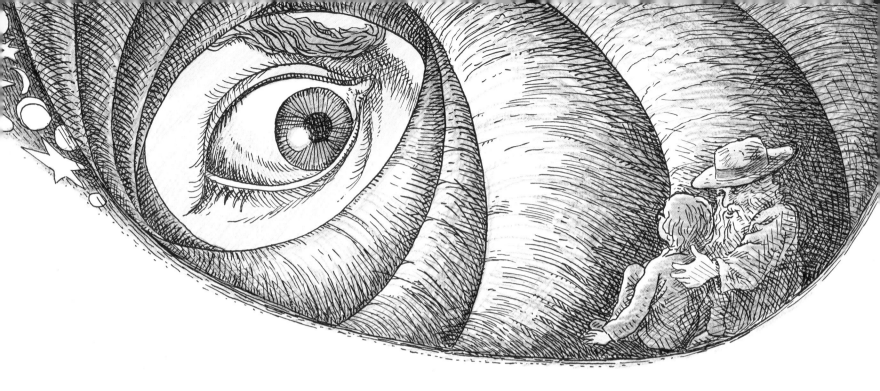

There they sat, and the Nap Master said, "No matter what scary things happen to you in the Land of Dreams, you'll always get away. So enjoy yourself and don't be afraid."

But an evil pirate-eye looked down at them, and a cruel voice said, "Into the drink with ye, then!"

The shell went flying from the pirate's hand and sank into the sea.

"Nap Master!" cried Herman. "We'll drown!"

"No, you won't. Just look down."

Herman looked. His feet and legs were turning into a curving tail.

"I'm a sea horse!" he shouted, and he swam out of the shell.

Eight long arms came wriggling after him. It was the Nap Master, who had changed into an octopus!

Now came a mysterious sea serpent (or saw serpent, whichever you prefer) with a light bulb on its tail and a saw at the end of its head.

"Nap Master, help!" shouted Herman as the sea serpent tried to saw off his tail.

"That's only the maintenance man having a dream," said the Nap Master, yawning.

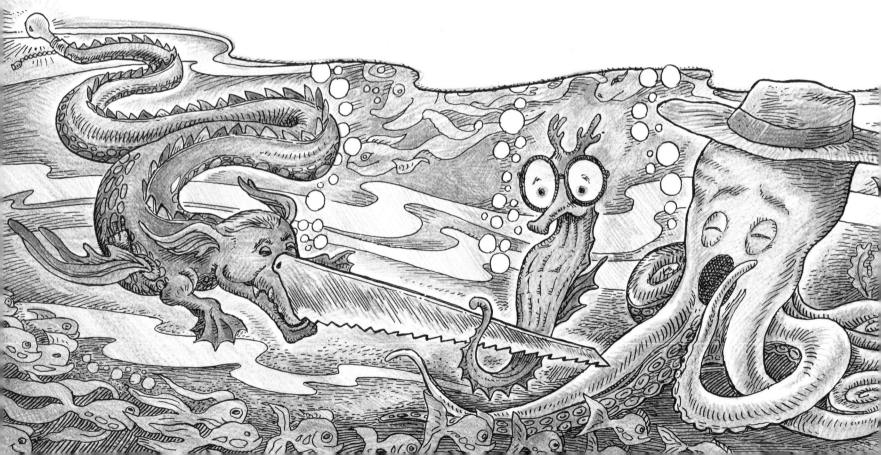

Every creature here is just someone's dream, thought Herman,
swimming toward an enormous castle.

The castle was filled with lost treasures of the sea.

Inside, a lovely mermaid danced.

Just then a diving bell came down. "Going up!" It was the elevator man. "But don't go pressing all the buttons or we'll wind up in the clouds."

As soon as the elevator man turned his back, Herman pressed all the buttons.

Up they went, up and up, into the clouds. "Someone," said the elevator man, "pressed all the buttons."

The wind blew them along, high above the Ocean of Dreams, until the Nap Master punched his finger through the cloud.

"Going down," he said, and suddenly they turned into raindrops, falling on the city.

"There's my building!" shouted Herman. "We're going home!"

He splashed on the window sill of his playroom, and the
next thing he knew he was awake in the big stuffed chair.

His mother came in, sleepily rubbing her eyes. "What a
nice dream I had," she said. "But I'm sorry to see the Nap
Master left without getting you to take a nap."

"Naps are for saps," said Herman.

But on the very next day, he took a nap without being
told. And inside his dream was the Nap Master, waiting for him.
They walked along together, down the winding Path of Dreams.